Rock-a-Baby Band

by Kate McMullan

Illustrated by

Janie Bynum

Megan Tingley Books
Little, Brown and Company
Boston New York London

For baby rocker, MiMi Knolle

— K. M.

To Taylor, my very own Rock-a-Baby

— J. B.

Text copyright © 2003 by Kate McMullan
Illustrations copyright © 2003 by Janie Bynum
Music by Paul Hodes, Copyright © 2003 by Big Round Music, LLC
Rock-a-Baby Band performed by Peggo and Paul with the Peggosus Band
℗ 2003 by Big Round Music, LLC

First Edition
Library of Congress Cataloging-in-Publication Data
McMullan, Kate.
Rock-a-baby band / by Kate McMullan ; Illustrated by Janie Bynum. — 1st ed.
p. cm.
Summary: Ten babies sing, dance, and use a variety of instruments to make music together.
ISBN 0-316-60858-0
[I. Babies — Fiction. 2. Music — Fiction. 3. Stories in rhyme.] I. Bynum, Janie, ill. II.
Title.
PZ8.3.M238 Ro 2003
[E] — dc2l   2002016178
10 9 8 7 6 5 4 3 2 1
IP
Printed in Singapore
The illustrations for this book were done in digital watercolor.
The text was set in Kidprint, and the display type was hand lettered by Janie Bynum.

One baby, two baby, three baby, four,

Five baby, six baby,
seven baby, more,

Eight baby,
nine baby,
ten baby,

and . . .

Put your hands together
for the
Rock-a-Baby Band!

Charlotte plays the rattle,

Denny plays the drum,

Bip and Ling have bells to ring.
HERE THEY COME!

Oh, shake it, baby, shake it!
Shake it if you can.

Shake it, baby, shake it
with the Rock-a-Baby Band.

Charlotte JANG, JANG, JANGLES,
Denny BAM, BAM, BAMs,

Bip and Ling
ring DING, DING, DING,

Backup babies jam!

Oh, shake it, baby, shake it
Shake it if you can.
Shake it, baby, shake it
with the
Rock-a-Baby Band.

Charlotte boogie-woogies,
Denny stomps and claps,

Bip and Ling begin to sing: "Rockers don't take naps!"

Oh, shake it, baby, shake it
Shake it if you can.
Shake it, baby, shake it

with the
Rock-a-Baby Band.

Charlotte spins and rattles,
Denny whirls and drums,

Bip and Ling twirl as they sing:
"Love to suck my thumb!"

Oh, shake it, baby, shake it!
Shake it if you can.
Shake it, baby, shake it

Charlotte's
getting dizzy,
Denny loops around,

Bip and Ling start giggling.
They all fall down!

One baby, two baby, three baby, four,
Five baby, six baby toppled on the floor,

Seven baby, eight baby, nine baby, ten —
How can the babies
ever rock and roll again?

Charlotte rolls and rattles,
Denny rolls and rocks,

Bip and Ling roll, ring, and sing:
"Don't step on my new blue socks!"

Oh, shake it, rock it, roll it,
Baby, if you can!

Shake it, rock it, roll it
with the
Rock-a-Baby Band!